I0623017

# THE DARK SIDE OF THE SUN

## HARPER M. TREMBLAY

THE WHUMPY PRINTING PRESS

Cover Illustration by Hen Towers

Cover Design by Nicole Alessi

To the best friend I've ever had and the strongest mother anyone could ask for — I love you.

# CONTENTS

— • —

# CONTENT WARNINGS

This story contains the following content:

- Torture, including unethical scientific experimentation

- Slavery

- Captivity

- Suicidal ideation

- Terminal illness

If this book isn't for you, no worries! But if it is, we hope you enjoy this story about an unexpected reunion...

—·—

"Do you know why you're here before me, Cassius?"

The creature looking down at Cassius was an ugly thing. Few of King Myndill's kind truly remained pure, but King Myndill was a fearsome creature indeed. His lupine amber eyes marked by the blackness of Taint never ceased to glow. His long, saber-tooth-like teeth stood out, even when he took that regal human form.

Cassius dared not face King Myndill's true form. Even just the silhouette of a large wolf could send villages fleeing in fear – for good reason too. That creature brought destruction wherever his dirtied paws found purchase.

"You're a fucking revenge-driven bastard, Myndill. I know you hate me and my kind. What, am I just your latest revenge piece? I know how you are."

Anger flashed in those charred eyes of his. "Watch your fucking mouth, Cassius."

The guards that held his arms down quickly pushed Cassius to the floor, agonizingly so. It took everything in Cassius not to give Myndill the satisfaction of a cry.

"I have much worse in mind for you than 'revenge,' dear Cassius." King Myndill used the edge of his boot to tilt Cassius' chin up in his direction. "You hate *my* kind. I know that well."

"Who wouldn't hate your kind? You were punished by the Judge for what you did. You're all rotten."

Myndill grinned wildly. "Most of us are here for very similar reasons to the suffering that you've imparted on others, Cassius. You're just lucky." Myndill used his boot to twist Cassius' head to the side. Then his boot came crashing down on Cassius' jaw. If his jaw hadn't immediately fallen out of place, Cassius might've screamed. "Don't forget who owns *your* life now."

Cassius let out a stifled groan. He couldn't move his jaw. It was an injury easily fixed with alchemy, but that didn't take away the humiliation of the moment.

"I don't plan on ever letting you go, Cassius. After a certain time, everyone's going to assume that I've killed you. I don't have such a merciful fate in mind for the likes of you."

Cassius let out a small growl as he narrowed his eyes at the King of the Tainted. He tired already of the creature's games. It was all overdone hysterics, anyway. Though Myndill was a fearsome creature, many of the other Tainted could overthrow him easily.

At least, that's what Cassius thought from his research. The Tainted each held a fearsome might. Every specimen he got his hands on seemed to be increasingly powerful. He wondered how this king even stayed in power. Most had to be afraid, he thought. Yet the king hadn't attacked any villages in the past hundred years on his own. That, to Cassius, was just a show of weakness and insecurity.

"Oh, it'll be so much fun to make you beg at my feet for scraps of that precious food you humans find yourself needing oh-so-very often."

Cassius doubted that Myndill would ever make him beg for anything.

"You'll regret ever crossing one of us, dear Cassius. You'll regret ever insulting me. You'll be one of the toys I'll enjoy shattering the most. I might even keep you longer. You'll last longer than most of the other toys I've had, after all."

That much was true, at least. Cassius knew his body could last many more days than most. He never planned on spending those days with a sick bastard like Myndill. No, he wouldn't waste his precious life with that false idol.

\*\*\*

Screams soon filled the halls of the palace. Hakon was far used to it after fifty years as a Tainted. He was lucky enough to have come under the protection and kindness of the king. Somehow, those fifty years he'd spent in that Tainted body of his, under the rule of a king he once found to be a beast of his night terrors, were the best of his life.

Today, though, something *felt* different. He was more acute to emotions now as a Tainted. How could he ever get used to hearing and feeling everything around him? It gave him headaches and overloaded him often when he was in crowds. The king had assured him that it was because he was only recently taken over by Taint.

Hakon begged to differ.

Memories of his time as a human came back to him easily when he heard those screams.

"Hakon?"

The Tainted next to him – a gentle fellow that Hakon was close to calling a friend – looked him in the eyes. "Are you okay?"

Hakon shook his head. "I thought I recognized the voice of His Majesty's new toy."

His friend was eerily quiet. Hakon's stomach dropped.

"You probably do, Hakon."

Hakon looked at his friend in confusion. Fear swarmed in his head, stinging his mind like hornets. "N-none of the humans I knew are alive anymore. If they are, they're too old for His Majesty's tastes in toys."

His friend shook his head. "I'll let His Majesty tell you him-self. He requested to see you before you go about your regular duties for today."

"What? You know!? Tell me! Tell me before I see him!" He couldn't hide the panic from his voice.

"I can't disobey His Majesty's orders, Hakon. You should see him as soon as you can, if you're so anxious."

Hakon nodded. He forced himself to take a deep breath, to focus on his heart beating in his chest as he held it. Once he'd brought his entire mind to his heart, letting his breath go through his mouth in a long, gracious stroke, his lungs seemed to fill more. His heart began to slow.

"Thank you. I'll see you soon." Hakon gave his friend a small smile, then went to his rooms to put on the necklace that his king had given him all those years ago.

\*\*\*

King Myndill's blood sang with wine and lust as he awaited Hakon's arrival on his throne. He wasn't quite deep in his cups yet, but he was certainly going to be. Whether because of cel-ebration of Cassius' capture or because he genuinely enjoyed the bottle he found himself drinking, Myndill didn't know. He wasn't sure he cared either.

Hakon came quickly once that friend of his had passed along the message. He came dressed in ceremonial robes, a scarf tied over his eyes. On his neck, Hakon bore the necklace he was always polite enough to wear when around Myndill.

Indeed, Hakon was a treasure as the Chaplain of the palace and the Seer of his kingdom. Few Tainted had the magic he did. He needed not sight nor smell to know where he was. His mind's eye was acute enough to guide him.

Not too many paces forwards or too many back, Hakon fell to his knees in a bow to his king. Myndill smiled. *A valuable asset, indeed.*

"You may rise, Hakon."

Hakon stood and bowed at the waist. "Yes, Your Majesty."

Myndill didn't need Hakon's magic to know that the young Tainted had a grave question on his mind. "What is it, Hakon? You may speak freely."

A look of surprise washed over Hakon's face. "Your Grace, I've had the feeling that I might know your new toy. Something tells me who he is and – I recognize his screams. His voice."

Myndill smiled. He hadn't told Hakon about Cassius' presence purposefully. Though it felt a little cruel to give the boy such a test, Myndill needed to know the strength of Hakon's magic – and the strength of his resolve. Myndill always had a sense that Hakon had an acuity that other Western-bound souls didn't have.

The resolve remained despite the tremor in the boy's voice.

"Who did you think it might be?"

Hakon looked hesitant, afraid almost. It wasn't unusual with the Tainted, for them to have been hurt by others before. Few were the Tainted whose sin was entirely random. Myndill was used to it by now.

"All is well, Hakon. You may speak to me. You're a valuable part of the palace. You don't have to fear others like you did when you were human."

Something flashed on that gentle skin of Hakon's. "I thought it might be Cassius. The one who – "

Hakon's voice caught and struggled on the words, so Myndill held his hand up.

"I understand, Hakon," Myndill soothed. "Indeed, I've taken Cassius as my new toy. He'll be fun to break. Imagine – the one who's hurt us for the past hundred years groveling at our feet for scraps of food. It'll be a long time before I get there with him. The day it comes, though, will be glorious."

A small smile parted Hakon's lips. The idea pleased him too.

"He's a bastard. He deserves everything he has coming at him, Your Majesty."

Myndill laughed a hearty laugh as he looked at Hakon. Despite his covered eyes, Hakon was able to meet his gaze. "He deserves every last part of it. I had the guards start him off easy today – we branded him to ensure that if he escapes our territory, he's returned immediately."

Hakon's smile faded a bit, turning into that shy smile of his early days at the palace.

"I know it's a sensitive subject, my dear Hakon. It's for his own good. He'd be killed instead of returned if he didn't bear our mark."

Hakon grimaced. "All the better. The world is better off without him, Your Highness."

Myndill smiled a bit, lapping up that little bit of defiance he'd cultivated in Hakon like a thirsty dog would water.

"I understand your wish, Hakon. I think that seeing him break first will be the perfect punishment for what he's done to us. Death would be a mercy for someone like him. He has two hundred years ahead of him, at least. Plenty of time to make sure he suffers before he dies."

Hakon nodded. "I am forever your loyal servant, My Lord."

Myndill smiled and stood from his throne. He ruffled Hakon's hair a bit. Admittedly, the boy was something of a son to him, even though such a relationship didn't exist in Tainted society or the one he came from. Where that paternal energy came from fascinated Myndill, even if the origin of the idea planted so deeply in his mind baffled him.

"I know you are, my dear. I couldn't be more thankful to have you around here. You're an invaluable asset to this kingdom and very dear to me." Myndill took a breath. "I imagine you'll want to see him."

Again, Hakon nodded. "Yes, Your Majesty."

Myndill hummed. "I want you to walk there with someone you trust." He held a finger up to shush the comment he was sure Hakon had. "I'm worried about how it'll affect you to see the one who made you the way that you are. They don't need to go into the room with you. They just need to wait outside for you and get you back to your rooms."

It was one of those genuine, unselfish concerns that Myndill had. They were rare, but not as much with Hakon.

"I'll survive. I've survived worse, Your Highness."

"I know you have." Myndill looked at the stained glass of his throne room. "I know you have, Hakon. You're strong. Stronger than you know. My goal as your liege is to have you save that strength, not to have you expend it on fools. If you need anything, you know that you can call on me, right?"

Hakon gave a small nod. "As you wish, Your Majesty."

Myndill smiled softly at him. "We're keeping him in the dungeons. You're welcome to come and go as you please. The guards all know who you are already."

A smile crossed Hakon's face. "Thank you, Your Majesty."

"Of course. Take good care of yourself. You are to make sure you have someone the first time. I don't mind if you touch him or anything this time. He's yours as much as he is mine."

"Thank you for your kindness, Your Majesty. I would like to go see him now."

"Of course. Make sure you eat something tonight too. You're looking thin."

Hakon chuckled and smiled. "I always look thin, Your Majesty. I had consumption as a human."

"Then it'll be easier to eat!"

The two laughed before Myndill gave Hakon a pat on the shoulder. "Take good care, my dear."

\*\*\*

The dungeons were a musty place. Cassius immediately hated it there, though he had more pressing issues than his running nose.

Rage flared in his mind every time the brand on his side ached from the rough handling of the guards. He wanted to punch them. He wanted to fight back.

It was a stupid idea to do either, though. Cassius knew better. Neither guard found a punch to the side. The brand would limit his movement for days and his jaw was somewhat broken.

*Once I'm alone, I need to see if I can fix my jaw.*

Broken bones were surprisingly easy to fix with alchemy. They were all minerals, something that alchemy excelled at changing. Skin made of human flesh, on the other hand, was not easy to fix. It was too complex compared to the simplicity of bone cells.

Once the guards had dumped him on the mossy, slightly damp floor of the cell, Cassius wasted no time meditating. His focus had to be unshakeable. The most pressing matter was fixing his jaw. *Then I need to destroy those stupid motherfuckers.*

Just as Cassius had gotten a feeling for the weather patterns in the area – a good pattern too, with lots of wind – he heard a familiar voice.

"Triple Onyx Cassius. I never expected to see you again, much less here of all places."

Cassius immediately lost all his focus as he looked out into those familiar honey-gold eyes, now lined with the black Taint of his kind.

"Elijah?"

The face of the Tainted before him changed. "I'm not Elijah anymore." His eyes narrowed. "I'm Hakon now. After what *you* did."

Cassius smiled a bit. "Hakon now, eh? Well, then, I see you've become one of my greatest successes if you've actually become one of the Tainted."

His words only seem to twist that once-innocent face more. It hurt him more than he cared to admit to speak with a half-fixed jaw, but the anger rolling off the Tainted like waves and filling the room was worth every second of pain.

"Shut the fuck up. I'm here because of my own decisions, not your stupid fucking experiments."

That only seemed to make Cassius smile more.

— ◦ —

Seeing Cassius smiling and laughing at him brought Hakon right back to those days in Cassius' lab with a needle in his arm. He forced himself to swallow the lump in his throat as he looked at his former captor, shirtless and sitting in cheap breeches.

The brand, King Myndill's mark, burned red and hot on his side. Of course, he was an alchemist and would be able to fight off infection much more easily. Hakon was still surprised to see that the brand wasn't covered.

Somehow, as he was watching Cassius smile from the ground, he found himself regarding the sight as rather pathetic. *This* was the man who'd tortured him? *This* was the man who'd kept him captive and made him accept punishment by the Judge?

The notion filled Hakon with rage he thought himself hardly capable of.

In fact, it made him want to punch that smirk right off of Cassius' stupid, smug face.

"Somehow, I doubt that quiet little Elijah managed to grow up into a big bad monster all on his own."

"Shut up. Shut up right now, you bastard!"

Cassius gave him that smirk he knew all too well. It only served to make Hakon angrier.

"What? Was it really all bad? Come on, if you want to hit me, go ahead. Hit that stupid fucking brand Myndill put on me. If it really was *that* bad with me, show me how angry it made you."

From his position above, Hakon soon realized that he was giving Cassius control over the situation. He hated how easily he'd let Cassius put him right back into that position he was all those years ago – fifty-five, now, wasn't it?

He wanted to beat the shit out of Cassius. Hakon wasn't the weak child that Cassius had tortured anymore. In fact, he was stronger than Cassius. Hakon didn't rely on hurting others for his self-esteem. Hakon knew he was powerful – probably stronger than Cassius, in fact.

It left him with a sense of pity for his captor. Part of him was angry that he was so weak back then as to let such a pathetic man torture him. Part of him knew it wasn't his fault – just like King Myndill had taught him.

Yet, because Hakon was stronger than Cassius in spirit and in magic, it was easy for him to figure out what he wanted to do.

"You're pathetic," Hakon spat. "Here you are, on the floor. You think you still have power over me. You still somehow think that taunting will get you anywhere. You see, Cassius, I'm not that person you knew all those years ago. I've become the

Seer for His Highness, King Myndill. In my presence, you will address him with respect."

Cassius scoffed.

"I pity you."

Cassius' face changed. That simple phrase had wiped the smirk off of his face with more grace and ease than any punch to the face would've.

"You pity me?" Cassius asked incredulously.

"You're a sad, pathetic worm of a man, Cassius."

Hakon pulled a small knife out of his boot. Cassius looked at Hakon with a glint of fear, entirely unsatisfying fear, in his eyes. Hakon didn't want Cassius to fear him, not anymore. Cassius' fear would not heal the hurt in his heart. It was best to leave that fear as a bitter taste in his mouth.

With the knife, Hakon cut a strip of fabric from his plain, white robes. He didn't really mind, in all honesty. What he was about to do was worth more than any old robes he'd thrown on to go see Cassius.

"Stay still, Cassius. I'll be able to see what you're going to do before you do it."

As Hakon reached to open the door of the cell, Cassius snapped like a rabid dog. "What the hell do you think you're doing? Are you trying to dress my fucking wound? Just who do you think you are?"

"I'm not sure who I am. I never was. Probably never will be. I might have you to thank for that. I don't know." Hakon took a deep breath. "I know one thing, though. You're weak and you're injured. You need my help."

"If I'm so weak and pathetic, what does that make you?" Cassius hissed. "I broke you so beautifully back then. A weak little orphan, suddenly an adult and alone in the real world."

Cassius' question gave Hakon pause. Still, Hakon continued in silence. Bafflingly, Cassius let him dress his brand wound. Hakon had never expected him to stay still.

"I'm not sure what it makes me." Hakon wrapped the bandages around Cassius' torso, pulling them snug, but not too tight. Cassius flinched in pain and groaned each time a new layer was added. "But *this*." He motioned to the bandages. "This makes me stronger than you."

To that, Cassius had no answer. Instead, Cassius let Hakon finish dressing his wound, then allowed Hakon to help him relocate his jaw.

"I know you can fix the rest with alchemy."

Cassius nodded.

As Hakon turned to leave, Cassius muttered something from behind him. "Seer suits you well, Hakon. You were always so observant."

Hakon said nothing as he walked back up the stairs. The comment made him feel a little sick. Why, he wasn't sure.

\*\*\*

Cassius spent longer than he would care to admit thinking about his conversation with Hakon.

The boy was so different from the orphan he'd taken in. Back then, he was a rather scared boy who was just barely an adult and had to face the horrors of the world on his own. People of that stripe made amazing prey for research subjects. Nobody would miss them. Nobody would ever even look for them. Nobody would lash out at the alchemists for keeping someone like that.

Back then, he was Elijah, with not even a family name to call his own.

The day they met, it was raining in sheets. Elijah had been sitting under the roof of the back entrance of a church – the entrance to the soup kitchen. He was thin and had the biggest bags under his honey eyes.

Cassius had been looking for someone to test an idea on. He'd managed to purify the bone marrow of a Tainted he'd killed with an affinity for curses. All that was left was to try injecting it in the corresponding organ area of someone else. Cassius had a theory back then that because mages stored their magic in organs, Taint originated in the same area.

Taint spread like a blight from person to person. One day, after an ill deed, people would turn into depraved, evil fae creatures with black sclera. They always reported a strange dream before Taint took over – at least, the ones that would or could talk to Cassius about their experiences.

Sometimes, Taint would infect an entire household. Cases were rare of a Tainted spreading their corruption, but it was typically in mage families with similar magic that it happened.

Thus, Cassius thought that if he could identify the direction of the soul of his subject and inject the purified version of the Tainted's bone marrow, he could corrupt their soul and create "artificial" Tainted.

His theory would prove deadly for many, so someone like Elijah was the perfect target. No alchemist accomplished much of anything without a few sacrifices along the way.

"You look hungry."

Elijah had perked up immediately. Cassius was holding an umbrella over his own head. It made him look particularly well-off.

"Sir, if you have any change to spare, I'd like to buy a warm meal. The soup kitchen only serves food once a day."

A small smile crawled onto Cassius' lips. He knew it made him look friendly to the scared child at his feet.

"Come, I'll feed you. You look so awfully thin."

Elijah shook his head. "S-sir, I can't. I have consumption. You'll catch it from me if you take me in."

"Consumption doesn't scare me." Cassius prepared himself to tell his little lie. "My brother had it and I grew up with him. I never caught it. I doubt you could give it to me if my own brother didn't."

That convinced Elijah.

"Tell me your name, child?"

"I-I'm not a child. I just turned eighteen three months ago." He ducked his head as he trailed behind Cassius when he started walking. "I'm Elijah."

Cassius nodded. "Eighteen is still very much a child. I'm Cassius. I'm an alchemist. I can help you, though. We aren't bad people. Lots of nasty rumors out there."

It was the honest truth. *Alchemists* weren't bad people. He wasn't a bad person, either, though he knew some would disagree. Some simply envied a man in the pursuit of knowledge. Not everyone had the stomach to handle when the pursuit of knowledge wasn't as noble as most thought it to be. It was a fact of life.

Little did Elijah know at the time that he would never step foot near that church again. Elijah would become something much greater than a street urchin.

Cassius thought he wasn't capable of regret. Yet seeing Elijah, now Hakon, a Tainted just like he'd intended all those years ago, filled him with an indescribable emotion that *hurt*.

Was that what regret felt like?

Cassius wasn't sure.

\*\*\*

King Myndill waited with a giddy sort of pleasure for his new toy to arrive. Cassius was a fighter, though that was more of a perk than the point. Cassius was a nuisance. Better a toy than a nuisance, King Myndill presumed.

Of course, his new toy came kicking and biting the guards like a feral beast. King Myndill smiled. *Perfect.*

"Leave him unrestrained and exit."

The guards bowed and shut the door to Myndill's personal torture chambers. The walls were lined with cabinets that held all sorts of materials he needed for his pets – materials to feed them, hurt them, and heal their wounds, eventually.

How would Cassius react today?

"That little shit Hakon came to visit me last night."

Of course, King Myndill knew already. He'd prepared time for him and Hakon to speak about how it had gone. "Hmm? What happened to make you so angry?"

A look of annoyance flooded Cassius' face. King Myndill had to stifle his chuckle. For such an arrogant man, Cassius certainly had never won a game of poker.

"You wouldn't believe it, but the little bastard still cares about me. He came and wrapped up my side, without your permission, I'm assuming."

King Myndill had noticed the bandages. He'd given Hakon permission to do what he pleased, so it didn't bother him. Hakon had a beautiful empathy within him. It was a gift – a helpful one at that. Seers needed empathy to be good at their jobs.

"I'm surprised he didn't just punch you in the face."

Cassius laughed. "Something we can agree on." Cassius got a wicked smile on his face. "He's oh-so-loyal to you, Your Royal *Highness*. He demanded that I call you by a proper title," Cassius scoffed.

"I was thinking about working on that with you, actually." A smile materialized on King Myndill's face. "Mocking me is a piss-poor idea, Cassius."

"If you want to see a piss-poor idea, just look at your kingdom."

King Myndill wasn't smiling anymore. That just egged Cassius on.

"Why take in a pathetic kid like that? When I had him, he could hardly wipe his ass without my permission."

"Keep speaking, Cassius, and I'll make you regret the day you were born."

Cassius took that as a challenge. "Really? Like I made *Elijah* regret ever being born?"

That was the end of King Myndill's rope. He threw a hard punch at Cassius' face, hitting him squarely in his already-injured jaw. A sharp kick to his abdomen, right on top of his brand, came next.

Cassius fell to the ground in a heap, coughing, biting back a scream of pain.

"Get up now. Face me."

Cassius didn't comply. King Myndill knew he couldn't.

King Myndill kneeled down and picked up Cassius' chin, tilting Cassius' head to watch the contorted look of pain wash over his face.

"Do not insult any Tainted, much less one as talented as Hakon, in my presence. They're like children, brothers, and sisters to me." He squeezed Cassius' jaw with his hand until Cassius was whimpering. "I'll make everything extremely clear to you, understand?"

King Myndill took a deep breath. "You will be *my* plaything from now until the day you die. If you're respectful and good, I'll treat you well. If you can't keep your damn mouth shut, you'll find yourself hurt. It's only natural. Humans don't understand anything other than pain."

Cassius scoffed, but King Myndill only squeezed his injured jaw more until the only noise he made was whimpering.

"From now on, dear Cassius, you have no god other than me. You will obey my every command. It'll take you a while to get there, I know, but you will. I promise you that I will learn every secret in your head, every horrible memory you'd rather forget, and every weakness you have."

Cassius, for the first time, had a horrible look of fear in his eyes. King Myndill smirked. "You know that I always make good on my promises, right?"

Cassius said nothing, but his silence confirmed that he was already beginning to break down a bit. He was starting to understand.

That just made King Myndill giddy as he prepared himself for what he would do with Cassius that day.

"You'll call me 'liege' before this day ends. However long that takes is your choice, Cassius, but it will happen."

The look of doubt on Cassius' face only served to make King Myndill more excited for what laid ahead.

— · —

Cassius lay there, freezing, on the ground of the torture room.

"Come on, dear, it's so easy. You can do well."

He hated that mocking tone of his captor – King Myndill. His body was littered with bruises and he was sure one of his ribs had cracked. Worst of all, the torture room of his captor was freezing cold and he was drenched with cold water.

Apparently, he'd needed a bath after the torture session, so King Myndill had taken to washing him by dumping a bucket of cold water on him.

Now –

"Come on, dear Cassius. All it takes is one word."

He was cold and naked and in desperate need of a towel. He was shaking, trying to warm up in any way possible. His wet breeches stuck to him, zapping away any heat his body could produce.

"Just call me 'liege' and I'll come to towel you off."

Myndill's smile was wicked. Cassius wanted to punch him in the face and wipe that smile right off of it. His one shoulder was almost certainly dislocated, and it ached, reminding him that he didn't want to tempt Myndill to break the other one.

"Look at you! You're sweating so much. Poor dear." Myndill clicked his tongue mockingly. "Do you need another bath?"

"No! I do not need more of that cold fucking water." Cassius' teeth were chattering, making it difficult to make out what he was trying to say.

"You don't need to be like this, Cassius. You're doing this to yourself. It's so easy. It's just one word to behave properly."

Cassius couldn't take the cold anymore. "My Liege."

Myndill hesitated. "Good boy."

His smile grew only more wicked and gleeful. Cassius hated it, but he was pathetically helpless. He was lucky that Myndill had decided against restraints, otherwise it would've been a lot worse.

Myndill tossed the towel to Cassius with a clean pair of breeches. "Get yourself dressed. I'll have someone bring you your food and water later."

***

Some types were more prone to Taint than others. The hedonists, like King Myndill himself, and the revenge-prone were always more likely to develop it than others.

Taint always fed off of those selfish, dark emotions. It was a double-edged sword – becoming a Tainted meant a life of never-ending persecution. Be that as it may, it also meant that those selfish, dark creatures no longer had to hide their darker self. In fact, that darker self was the source of a Tainted's power.

For King Myndill, becoming a Tainted had been a gift beyond measure. As a fae creature, he was always weak. As a Tainted, he was powerful. He stood above all others in pure strength.

With that power, he built a kingdom. His kingdom grew to such might that it could take land easily. His people were never without food. His people never suffered death at the hands of those who hated them. They could all sleep easily at night. King Myndill couldn't be more proud.

Despite King Myndill's best efforts, the Kingdom of the Tainted was missing many things. For one, they had little healing magic. Healing types almost never fell victim to Taint. It was only one of the numerous concerns of having a high concentration of individuals whose magic was largely destructive in nature.

King Myndill didn't know why he went out to collect the new Tainted that day. Had he thought to scare the creatures outside his kingdom? No, that didn't make sense.

That day was fifty years ago now – a short time to a five hundred year old creature, yes, but still long enough to lose memories.

It was a miserable day too. One of the worst blizzards King Myndill could remember had moved in. His patrols couldn't encounter any issues or else risk leaving new Tainted out to die. He preferred being out in the field, anyway, helping them. It was thrilling compared to royal life. He could let his wolf out too, and run like he didn't have a care in the world other than the mission.

They'd almost missed Hakon that day.

"Your Majesty, I think someone's in the snow!"

King Myndill stopped immediately. Patrol members hurried to begin digging in the snow. They could hardly see a few stone tosses in front of them, but the Tainted who'd found the young man was very talented in sensing the soul of another.

As it turned out, she was absolutely right.

A young man with black sclera and honey-gold eyes laid under the snow. His skin was flushed with frostbite.

"Get me some blankets!"

King Myndill allowed one of the patrol members to wrap the young man in blankets and lean him up against Myndill's warm, furry body.

"He won't be the only one. You can leave me with him here," Myndill ordered the patrol members. "I'll see if he can be saved."

The patrol members nodded. They wouldn't disobey the orders of their king.

They left Myndill with extra blankets. He didn't want them to linger.

From the look of the young man, Myndill figured he was probably once human, which meant that he would need a fae name.

"You look like a Hakon."

It was a fond name for King Myndill. He, admittedly, wasn't the best at sensing the nature of a person, but even he could tell that something was very different about the young man. King Myndill would later learn that he had one of the rarest magics of all for a Tainted – Western magic.

A small smile parted King Myndill's lips as he warmed the young man with his hot breath. He couldn't wait to meet this honey-eyed gift to his kingdom.

***

"How did your meeting with Cassius go yesterday?"

King Myndill sat at a table this time. Sometimes he and his consumptive Seer would eat together. Though neither of them really *needed* to eat, it was definitely more pleasant *to* eat than to use worldly energy to sustain themselves.

Hakon was hardly a consumptive anymore. He couldn't spread his disease nor would it progress beyond what it did while Hakon was human. He still sometimes suffered coughing fits and was always thin and pale, so Myndill did what he could to encourage him to eat regular meals, even if they weren't necessary for Hakon to survive.

After all, surviving wasn't living.

"It went well, Your Majesty."

Myndill knew that wasn't the whole truth.

Hakon, just as he was about to take a bite of his food, broke down in a coughing fit. Once Myndill was sure that he wasn't choking, he allowed Hakon to finish coughing.

"Sorry, Your Majesty."

Myndill shook his head. "No reason to apologize." He moved his food around before he decided on where to take a bite. "He said a lot of things."

Hakon froze, but Myndill gave a reassuring gesture. "It's okay. I won't go into details, but I see why you hate the bastard. You should've beaten him up. I would've understood."

Myndill loved the thoughtful look Hakon got when he was deeply considering what to say next. Quietly, Hakon ate a bit in between thoughts. That was one of his Seer's quirks. Eating and thinking didn't come as naturally to Hakon as it did to most.

"It felt wrong." Hakon put down his fork. "Wouldn't I be just as bad as him if I did that? I – I just can't imagine hurting him. I don't think that it's the way for me to reclaim power over my life. Not at all."

Myndill hummed a little. *You're an interesting Tainted, Hakon. What did you do to get to this place?*

"Hmm ... I'm not sure. That's a very personal question, Hakon." Myndill smiled at him, glowing a bit with pride. Hakon was young for a Tainted but held none of the youthful vengeance of a young Tainted. "I wouldn't have given him a lick of mercy. But I'm also Southern-bound. You're unique. You're Western-bound. Your soul wants different things from mine."

Hakon nodded. "Thank you, Your Majesty."

Again, that look.

Myndill stayed silent.

"If it's well with you, Your Majesty, I would like to keep visiting him. I don't think I can put my soul to rest until I find what it wants with him. It wants something, Your Majesty, and it will not allow me to lay in peace until it gets what it wants."

Myndill nodded, intrigued. "Of course, Hakon. You may visit as often as you want. You know his tricks better than I do. I know you'll be safe." Myndill took the last bite off of his plate. "I saw you tended to his wound. Would you like to try to bring him his meals? His water? He is still a human. I need him in good shape for what I want to do."

Hakon considered it for a long time. "Yes, Your Majesty. It would please me to give it a try."

Myndill smiled at Hakon. Glancing at Hakon's plate, he frowned. "You need to eat more."

Hakon couldn't help a chuckle. "Of course, Your Majesty."

\*\*\*

Hakon picked up the food for Cassius in the kitchen. The cooks definitely looked at him differently, but Hakon didn't care. He was the Seer, after all. The Seer never got a normal look from the Tainted around him. Uneasy, weary, suspicious looks. Sometimes ones of admiration or envy, maybe, but not the look of any passerby.

*Why did I agree to this? Why did I say that I wanted to see that bastard again?*

Hakon couldn't answer any of those questions.

He wanted more with Cassius, but what exactly he was hoping to accomplish was unclear.

*I wish I could cast a spell on myself.*

Sometimes, Hakon used his magic to help others make decisions. Perhaps cruelly, though, he could never use his magic on himself. At least, not spells like that. He could enhance his senses and the like, sure, but never help himself with anything practical.

A dangerous pang of self-doubt flared in his chest.

*I'm doing the right thing.* Hakon shook his head. *I'm doing the right thing. I just don't know what that is right now. I always figure it out.*

That was true. Whether with Cassius or with King Myndill, Hakon always figured something out.

Hakon took a deep breath.

*I'll be okay.*

After all, Cassius had no power other than the power that Hakon gave him now. Hakon wouldn't let Cassius have any power over his life. He wouldn't allow Cassius to take away what he had, not like in those days.

The guards moved aside quickly for Hakon. Even the guards in front of Cassius' cell were quick to leave in his presence.

A chuckle came from the cell.

"Aren't you quite the celebrity?"

Hakon knew that Cassius was grinning, even if he was hiding in the shadows. He could also see ...

*Wounds? His shoulder looks dislocated. Are his ribs okay?*

Hakon didn't know what he was expecting. Of course Cassius would go get himself beaten up by King Myndill. King Myndill didn't tolerate disrespect for authority. Hakon wasn't sure that Cassius even knew what authority *was*. Other than his own, maybe.

"They respect me." Hakon set the tray of food on the ledge of the cell made for such things. "Unlike someone I know."

Cassius raised his one hand as he limped out of the shadows. He looked worse than Hakon had expected. He had a black eye and a large bruise on his already-injured jaw. His left arm hung incorrectly from his shoulder.

Hakon felt a cough coming on. He quickly took out the cloth he kept in his pocket and coughed into it.

"Still a consumptive?" Cassius took the food from the ledge.

"Becoming a Tainted doesn't heal disease. It just prevents it from spreading and progressing."

Cassius looked genuinely surprised. Hakon smiled a bit. *He must not have known.*

It felt amazing to have known something that Cassius hadn't.

Cassius didn't admit it.

He never would have.

Hakon sat in silence against the wall for a while.

"Do you really need to stay here while I eat every bite of my food?"

Cassius' mood was quickly turning foul. Hakon might've scoffed if the sound of that irritation didn't send chills down his spine.

"I need to collect the tray."

"You seem a little high-ranking to be collecting dishes from me."

Hakon shrugged at the comment meant to agitate him. "I am. You're a special case."

Cassius grinned. Hakon hated the look of it.

"Do you want me to help you set that shoulder? It'll heal faster if I set it now."

Cassius' grin faded. A small smile of triumph split Hakon's mouth.

"No. I'll deal with it on my own."

Clearly, the question had soured his appetite. He returned the tray.

"The food's shit. Get me something better tomorrow."

—·—

Were the times with Cassius all bad?

The question haunted Hakon more often than he cared to admit. As he laid in bed, resting that morning, he found himself thinking back to that time when he was "Elijah."

Cassius kept him in a single bedroom with a small, doorless bathroom. The door to his tiny, cramped bedroom was always locked in the beginning. Cassius didn't trust him not to run.

Even with the benefit of hindsight, Hakon wasn't exactly sure why. He had nowhere to go. He was a consumptive orphan. Nobody would've taken him in, especially since he didn't have any job skills. His only hope would be to be sent to a sanatorium. Even then, nobody would believe that an alchemist kidnapped him and tortured him. They were too secretive.

That assumed he could even outrun the alchemist. His lungs simply might not hold.

Cassius, at some point, realized that Hakon wasn't going to run. One day, he'd actually asked why. Hakon had been naive enough back then to believe that the alchemist might've asked out of care.

His answer had changed everything.

Cassius had burst out laughing. "I can't believe I didn't think of that before!" He needed a moment to calm down from his laughter. "You're right. You couldn't run from me, even if you tried. At least I know where to drop you off if this experiment fails. I heard the sanatorium near here isn't bad. Maybe you should've gone there. I would've never come to get you."

Hakon didn't know why he was so hurt by Cassius' response. Cassius was an ass, of course. He always was, no matter the day. He should've expected the cruel response. He felt stupid for expecting anything else.

Of course, Cassius was also right. The alchemist was more acute than he gave himself credit for. Maybe Cassius hadn't realized it that day when Hakon had sat at the steps of the soup kitchen, fighting off a fever, but Hakon well and truly had nowhere to go. He'd slept on the streets before Cassius. At least he had a warm meal once in a while and a place to sleep with Cassius.

From then on, Cassius would *sometimes* allow Hakon out of his room between tests, so long as he didn't enter the kitchen or any of the other bathrooms. One night, he'd forgotten to lock Hakon back up. Hakon was smart, even back then, and knew not to anger Cassius. Thus, he'd decided to wake Cassius up.

He immediately took Hakon by the throat and squeezed until Hakon was coughing and spitting, struggling helplessly for air. Cassius' hands were going to leave bruises, Hakon was sure.

He squeezed a little tighter. "Don't you fucking dare watch me sleep."

With that, he dropped Hakon to the ground. Hakon was simply left in a coughing pile, using the cuff of his sleeve to cover his mouth. If Hakon didn't know that Cassius was largely immune to disease like consumption, he would've thought Cassius stupid for strangling a consumptive.

"Let's get you to your room before you cause any more problems for me."

"P-please let me finish coughing."

Cassius had thrown a sharp punch to Hakon's face in response. "I said get to your room. You have the audacity to not use a proper title for me too. I'll punish you for that." Cassius narrowed his eyes. "Since you're so worried about that disease of yours, how about I wash that mouth?"

The taste of the caustic combination of vinegar, lye, and alcohol lingered in Hakon's mouth as he fell asleep that night, afraid of seeing Cassius the next morning.

\*\*\*

Hakon happened upon a sleeping Cassius. Hakon never knew Cassius to be a particularly deep sleeper, but Cassius' body was injured and his mind was surely weary. Stubbornly refusing medicine would have only casted an even deeper sleep spell.

Cassius was sweating and his face was flushed. *Did his wound get infected?*

Cassius' weakness then made Hakon deeply uncomfortable. Fifty years ago – the years Hakon lived as a Tainted passed so quickly. In those years of unrivaled health, Hakon had forgotten that even powerful alchemists like Cassius suffered infection in deep wounds.

That familiar fear – the taste of the lye mix too – lingered in his chest. Waking Cassius felt like waking a rabid bear.

Even after working himself up over the task, Hakon didn't have to wake Cassius that day. As he opened the door to the tray-deposit ledge, Cassius stirred.

Hakon expected to see rage. Hakon expected Cassius to yell and admonish him for watching him sleep.

Instead, all Hakon got out of Cassius was a simple, "Wow, I was really asleep."

Wincing, he stood and came to get the food. Cassius, for perhaps just a moment, seemed human in his fatigue and pain.

"I hope you made sure that the food isn't shit today. If it still is, I'm going to tell that fucking king of yours that you're making me starve."

Hakon was quiet.

"He wouldn't touch me. He doesn't punish his subjects – not like you."

Cassius scoffed. "I beg to differ. I'm surprised you're so loyal to *His Majesty* when you were a total brat for me."

"You aren't one of his subjects. You're free game," Hakon retorted, though his heart wasn't in the insult.

Cassius gave Hakon a little look of surprise. "The food's still shit, by the way."

Hakon scoffed. "Glad to hear it."

Cassius gave a laugh that ended abruptly.

Neither of them said anything else until Cassius finished half his tray. "Going to let him know that you're intent on starving me."

"Go ahead. Who do you think he'll believe?"

Cassius scowled, but he said nothing.

A long moment of silence passed between them.

"The weather here is really turbulent."

It was Hakon's turn to be confused. *What does that have to do with anything?*

Cassius' eyes narrowed. "I need you to help me relocate my shoulder, dumbass. I think that brand he gave me is infected too."

Hakon was indignant. "That's some way to ask for help."

For once, Cassius had to swallow his pride. "I can't do it myself. My Source is atmospheric convection. The convection here is too unpredictable. I'm not used to controlling it. I hate this just as much as you do, Hakon. You're a pathetic, weak kid. I shouldn't have to stoop down to asking someone like you. But you offered last night, and at least you know what it is to fear me. I'm stubborn, but I'm not stupid. I know when I need help."

Hakon wanted to growl and hurl harsher words than he could think of at Cassius. He wanted to punch him and wipe that horrible smirk off of his face.

Yet something in him told him to help Cassius. Hakon didn't want to add to Cassius' misery, not the same way that Cassius had to Hakon's. He was so much better, so much stronger than Cassius now.

His heart didn't believe that.

"The thought of helping you makes me sick." Hakon sighed. "I'm going to help you either way. I don't enjoy watching others in pain."

"Whatever helps you sleep at night, *Tainted*."

Hakon knew the venom in those words well. "At least I'm not a bastard alchemist who kidnaps people to torture them."

Cassius frowned. "The progress of science won't be stopped by some Tainted with too many opinions."

A frustrated groan escaped Hakon as he entered the cell. Cassius stubbornly refused to stand to meet him, so Hakon had to kneel reluctantly. He knew Cassius could stand; what Cassius wanted was always more important. "Maybe don't say that to the person relocating your shoulder."

"Good idea."

The words caught Hakon off guard. Cassius wasn't being sarcastic. He tried to shake off the surprise, but it lingered as he took hold of Cassius' shoulder and gave it a strong push. Cassius let out a small cry of pain as his shoulder *snapped* loudly into place.

"Anything else?"

Cassius shook his head. "Unless that king of yours can change the weather, I don't need anything else." He motioned to the tray. "Take the food with you, busboy. I don't feel like getting up."

Hakon got up and picked up the tray, the potentially infected brand long forgotten. He hated obeying Cassius. He hated how easily it came to him. Most of all, he hated Cassius and his *attitude*.

It took all the self-control he had to hold back a punch as he left the cell.

\*\*\*

Hakon spent most of his time alone. The reason wasn't exactly that he enjoyed his own company, but that he found difficulty in the company of others. There was only one other person he trusted – a Tainted much older than him, Alfie.

Alfie worked in the stacks of the library most of the time. However, they and Hakon had found a certain kinship that pushed them to be Hakon's personal assistant during his Seer duties. That meant that Alfie fetched Hakon when it was actually time to perform his duties.

Sometimes, Alfie came to his quarters regardless. Always good company, Hakon welcomed the opportunity to have them around. Though they had about one hundred years on Hakon, they had the understanding to converse with someone much younger – and someone who had been human once; Alfie had been some genderless fae creature all those years ago. They looked up to Hakon and his role as Seer. They were exceptionally untalented with Western-bound magic, despite being Southwestern-bound themself.

The role of Seer actually afforded Hakon quite a lot of time off. Aside from his regular readings that took him at most three hours, he sometimes had to perform other readings or help with an interrogation. Those were somewhat rare occasions, so he spent a lot of time journaling and writing about what he read. Anything that could keep the outside world on the outside and his internal world inside of him.

"Hakon!"

Alfie always greeted him with a smile that reached their black-green eyes.

"His Majesty wishes for you to complete a special reading today. He wants it completed as quickly as possible. It sounds important."

Hakon nodded and stood up from his desk, placing his pen down gently. "Let me prepare."

"Of course."

Alfie waited patiently in the hardly-touched entertaining room of Hakon's quarters while Hakon prepared himself. He first drew the Seer's symbols on the palms of his feet and hands and over his heart. Then, careful not to smudge the wet ink, he closed his eyes and placed ink over them. Finally, he tied a blindfold over his eyes.

Slowly but surely, those golden threads appeared in his vision to guide him. They guided his feet through the marks on his palms and brought him to Alfie. In those golden threads, Alfie looked like a crocheted doll with hollow eyes. It was like that for all the Tainted – he could never see the eyes.

"I'm ready."

Alfie nodded.

Together, the two of them made their way down to the Seer's Library. Hidden deep underground, only the librarian and those who saw the threads could enter.

Some things in the world held on to the threads very well and were almost spools. At first glance, the daily task of unwinding the spools and detangling what they recorded from every corner of the world might seem like difficult but enthralling work. Yet to call it "work" would be deceiving. Hakon read the spools so quickly that he hardly noticed time passing.

"Which spool does he want me to work on?"

43

Alfie, with their gloves on, brought over a particular spool. It was made of bones from a Southeastern-bound soul, though perhaps a little aged. For some reason, their ability to linger persisted long after death and made their bones an excellent conduit for threads.

Quietly, Hakon put his fingers to the thread as Alfie left the room. Each string through the conduit was a link between him and the threads in a completely different area.

This one – Hakon recognized. He recognized it a little too well.

*An alchemist's college! What does he want me to read?*

Hakon ran his fingers up and down the thread, trying to see where in time King Myndill wanted him to read. Though it was possible to read the past with threads, the length of time he could go back depended on the strength of the conduit. Because of the state of the bone, Hakon could read back about a day, which only served to make his work harder.

That was until he happened upon what King Myndill probably wanted him to see.

"Cassius has been taken by King Myndill of the Tainted."

A group of alchemists shrouded by their robes and cloaks gathered in the center of a meeting room. Vaguely, Hakon recognized them. It took everything in him not to lose his focus as he continued his reading.

"If you ask me, he was asking for it. You would've gotten away with it two hundred years ago. Not today! King Myndill is simply too powerful, too defensive over his kin."

Someone else in the room scoffed.

"He was too reckless." *That was the leader, right?* "I don't know if we'll be able to rescue him. He's too far into Tainted territory. They would easily overwhelm us unless we received aid from the Hall or one of the Strongholds. I doubt we'd receive it because it isn't an act of aggression against alchemists, just against one person."

The other alchemists in the meeting room nodded.

"I think it's still worth a try, though. Cassius is reckless, but he's intelligent and has some of the best leads on Magnum Opus that we've had in centuries."

Again, the alchemists all nodded their agreement. A miasma of disdain, perhaps even hatred, hung in the room.

*They're agreeing because they have to.*

Hakon swallowed.

"I'll contact Valentina's Stronghold. She has experience fighting the fae."

"She's rather far to contact. Plus, she's still recovering from that assassination attempt. Couldn't we find someone on our continent?"

"There's nobody better than her."

They all nodded their agreement. The sense of closure among the alchemists told Hakon he could let go of the string. He felt nauseous and exhausted in a way that was simply different.

Alfie's concerned gaze hardly registered.

"Are you okay?"

Hakon shuddered, more disturbed by the image than he wanted to credit it for.

"Sorry. It was just – the reading was of one of the colleges I went to while Cassius held me captive."

Alfie nodded. "I'm the one who should be apologizing. Are you still able to read? Maybe it'll help you take your mind off of what you just saw."

Hakon thought over their question for a while. "I'll try."

After all, they both understood that the only way that Hakon coped with his flashbacks and disturbing memories was work.

*** 

"So they're too weak to attack us directly?"

The smile on King Myndill's face told Hakon everything he needed to know. King Myndill was talented in many realms of trickery – a poker face was not one of them. Perhaps it was because he'd spent a good portion of his life as a wolf. Regardless, he wasn't among that small pack of the last of his kind anymore. He was King of the Tainted.

"Yes, Your Majesty."

He chuckled gleefully. "Who's this Valentina character?"

Hakon took a deep breath. "From what I gather, she's a combative alchemist from another continent. I don't know which one, but to ask for her means that she has to be rather powerful."

King Myndill looked puzzled for a moment. "I'll need you to gather information on her. If they plan to have her help in attacking us, I want to know everything there is to know about her."

Hakon gave a dutiful nod. Even if watching alchemist society would be difficult for him, Hakon was the only Seer that the Tainted had. It was his responsibility to serve his kingdom in the way only he could.

King Myndill ruffled his hair as he sat there, waiting for more orders.

"You're a good man, Hakon. I'm proud of you. You've done very well for us. You've also grown more than I could've imagined. We're very lucky to have a strong, driven, and *kind* Tainted among us."

Hakon grinned, glowing at the praise. He could tell it was genuine. After all, King Myndill was more of a father than Hakon ever had. Cassius certainly had never filled that role, nor did any of the attendants at the orphanages.

"Thank you, Your Majesty."

"You're like a son to me, Hakon. Of course."

Sometimes, Hakon wondered if he would be in line for the throne. The relationship he had with Myndill was special. King Myndill had a will that included the name of his successor, but nobody had ever seen it.

The thought of going from an orphan to potentially a king always struck Hakon as terrifying. Would he want that position? Could he even handle it?

He found himself entirely unworthy, even if King Myndill had worked Hakon's whole life as a Tainted to change his warped view of himself. At his core, though, he was a weak kid that had been tortured and used for an experiment by an alchemist.

In King Myndill's eyes, that was a strength. In Hakon's eyes, it couldn't be more of a weakness. What would happen, come the day that the alchemists wanted more from the Tainted? Would Hakon even be able to stand up to them without being filled with terror?

What if they chose Cassius to lead them, knowing that Cassius was his one true weakness?

As King Myndill pulled Hakon into a warm embrace, Hakon forced himself to think about something else. Self-doubt was a dangerous emotion for someone like him. He needed to be confident to perform his duties.

*Anyway, that's a long time from now.*

King Myndill was too kind, too powerful, to fall so easily.

"Useless! Fucking useless!"

Cassius remembered well throwing down all his instruments under the fearful gaze of his experimental subject. He'd managed to get ahold of a mage's compass. He knew it was possible that Elijah didn't have any affinity for magecraft, but he didn't plan for *what* kind of magecraft Elijah would be talented in.

"You're fucking Western-bound."

His voice was a low hiss as he stared daggers into Elijah. Elijah whimpered pathetically on the table. He was completely immobilized, strapped down with leather onto Cassius' workbench. Cassius somehow doubted that he'd be moving, even if he wasn't strapped at practically every major joint.

"S-sir?"

"Didn't you hear me?" Cassius shouted. "I can't follow the fucking protocol. You're Western-bound. Do you have even the slightest clue what I'm talking about?"

Elijah shook his head fearfully. "No, I-I-I don't, sir." He sounded on the verge of tears.

Cassius growled his annoyance.

Everything about his experiment had fallen apart in an instant. It took everything inside himself to not pull Elijah off of the table and beat him to a pulp. The only two directions that would be difficult to inject with the serum he'd made were Northwest and West. Even then, he was sure he could manage Northwest. The heart was the only organ that was completely impenetrable.

Elijah watched him as he stormed over to his books, trying to figure out anything he could do. Cassius stared at those blood vessel charts for a long time. It would be incredibly risky to use a vein near the heart to access it, especially when he was unable to see anything.

He looked back at Elijah.

The kid could die if he attempted what he was thinking. Granted, there was a good chance that the Taint didn't take and he died regardless. Elijah *was* going to die in the next few years, anyway. He was consumptive. What did it matter if he died?

The idea didn't sit well with Cassius. Almost nothing stopped him. But this, cutting a conscious, terrified person – a twenty-something-year-old who might've become a mage – open for his own purposes pushed the limits of what he would do.

He stormed to the door of his lab and quickly shut it behind him.

"Somebody get me some fucking saline! And some piping."

The supplies arrived quickly afterwards. The ability to give fluids through a vein was a well-kept secret of the alchemists. It might've easily cured cholera and dysentery, if not for the fact that the alchemists didn't want people knowing what they really used it for – surgeries and experimentation.

Cassius didn't re-enter the lab until he had everything ready. He grabbed one of his bottles of whiskey just in case.

"Alright, kid, we're doing this."

He doused his hands in the whiskey, caring little for the bit of residue it left behind.

He offered the bottle to Elijah. "Do you want whiskey?"

Elijah froze. Cassius' patience eventually wore thin while Elijah laid there, anxious and unable to put words together to answer him. Cassius said nothing as he took a swig of whiskey and headed over to the supplies.

In theory, the Taint would target Elijah's heart. Therefore, if Cassius injected the serum directly into a vein with saline, he might be able to test his theory. He wouldn't have to use a catheter to enter his heart that way. It would be a lot less dangerous of a procedure.

As he prepared Elijah for the infusion, Elijah gave him a panicked look.

*He had his chance for pain relief.*

Cassius attached extra straps to Elijah's right arm. He couldn't have Elijah moving.

"Stay. Still."

The warning was enough. Elijah froze again as Cassius quickly placed the needle and hurried to hook him up to the saline.

The drip started soon enough. Through the access port, Cassius injected Elijah with the Taint serum slowly.

The screams that came from Elijah over the next few hours still haunted Cassius. He wasn't one to be haunted by such a thing, but the nerves of potentially succeeding combined with the heartbreakingly shrill tone of Elijah's screams were what made the sound *stick*.

Did he regret it?

He didn't regret the pain he put Elijah through, even if it was all for nothing in the end. No, he only regretted that the experiment had failed. Elijah had remained human.

***

The question still bothered Cassius – if his experiments hadn't turned Hakon into a Tainted, then what had?

Cassius knew it was poor taste to ask a Tainted what had caused them to succumb to Taint, but he felt his relationship with Hakon was just ... different. It still wouldn't be polite, but after what he'd done, he felt he had a right to know.

Dinner was when Hakon stayed the longest. He always looked a little tired when bringing Cassius his dinner. If Cassius remembered correctly, when Hakon was tired, he tended to answer questions more easily.

*Fifty years didn't seem so long before.*

When Cassius thought about it, those fifty years were about a quarter to a sixth of his life. The thought didn't bother him, exactly. His memory of that time with Hakon was so clear that it just didn't feel like a quarter of a lifetime ago.

"I've been meaning to ask you," Cassius started. Hakon looked up at him with that delightful distaste. "What exactly made you a Tainted?"

Hakon scoffed. "What makes you think I would tell you? Don't you know it's awfully rude to ask a Tainted what made them succumb?"

"Well, I just wanted to know." Cassius shrugged a bit. "I wanted to know who your maker is if it isn't me. If you don't tell me, I guess I can just assume that I really did succeed. You'll have been my biggest success. When I get out of here, I can get another subject and just repeat what I did with you."

Cassius knew that Hakon fell for taunts easily.

"You aren't my fucking maker."

Cassius could tell by the rage in Hakon's eyes that he was about to tell him exactly what he wanted to hear.

Hakon took a deep breath. "I'll make a deal with you. I know you alchemists can at least hold a promise." He gave an expectant look, to which Cassius nodded. "I'll tell you how it happened, because for years I've wanted to tell you how you ruined any chance I ever had at being happy as a human, then you'll tell me why the fuck you did what you did."

It wasn't as weighty of a promise as Hakon clearly believed it to be. "I promise to give you the honest answer, if you're honest with me."

Reasons were in no short supply.

"I don't even know why I'm telling you this," Hakon muttered. "The day after you let me go, I ended up in a bad street fight. You see, people knew something was wrong with me. It wasn't the scars or how scared I looked. They felt the remnants of the Taint that you put in me."

Cassius stayed quiet, intrigued. He'd let Hakon – Elijah, then – go a few months after his final experiment with the Taint failed.

"I didn't trust any decision I made. I was scared that the Taint was warping my mind. I was scared that it would turn me into an evil person. I couldn't trust myself. Still, someone tried to be my friend. She was kind and smart and so, so tough. She was also a consumptive, like me."

Hakon took a sharp breath. Cassius did his best to look entertained. The backstory didn't matter. He wanted to know the moment it happened.

"You see, Cassius, succumbing to Taint doesn't happen all at once."

Cassius couldn't keep the look of shock off his face. Hakon only sadly smirked.

"I couldn't make any decisions. I was swallowed entirely by self-doubt. I couldn't tell the truth from the lies anymore. As you know, Western-bound souls need to have a good sense of self. We can't suffer in self-doubt nor lose sight of what's important. I'd done just that.

"One day, we got into a street fight. She died because I froze. I couldn't trust myself to not die in the process of saving her. You see, Cassius, indecision is as much of a decision as any of those decisions you've made. I learned that the hard way."

That struck Cassius into silence. A pang of something that resembled guilt struck him, but he quickly pushed it aside.

"One night, I had a nightmare. An odd woman came to visit me in my dreams and told me that my soul had been swallowed by its weakness. You see, every soul, depending on its direction, has an emotion it loses itself to. Mine was self-doubt. She warned me that I needed to turn myself in to those who bring the Tainted to King Myndill's kingdom. That they would protect me to the border."

"That was the Judge."

Hakon nodded. "She isn't a judge at all. She just ... she warns us. She tells us what happened to us. She guides us."

Cassius couldn't help a small laugh. "The gods don't forsake you after all."

"If anyone was forsaken by the gods, it's you."

Cassius went quiet again. He hated the power that Hakon had over his words. The man could make him speechless like none before. Nothing made him angrier.

"Well, you wanted to know why I took you, right?"

Hakon nodded, hesitant.

"You were so pathetic there on the ground that day. I figured nobody wanted you. I was right too, it seems. I'd had a theory I wanted to test for a while, but I didn't have anyone to test it on. You were just too perfect to pass up. All I had to do was offer you food. I knew that you could disappear and nobody would care if you never showed up again."

Cassius took a small, dramatic breath. "See, I don't let anything as silly as principles stop my research. Some alchemists have more principles than me – most of them do, in fact. But I don't think that's the right way to go about things. You were perfect. I did what I did because you were a means to an end, nothing more, nothing less. Like I told you before, nothing personal."

Hakon was quiet for a very long time. "You've said that all before. You couldn't be more wrong." There were tears in Hakon's eyes. "There are a lot of people who want me here. They value me. I'm the Seer. I can look at the past, present, and future of *any* part of the world. I'm stronger than you ever were. I overcame the weakness of my soul."

Hakon looked up at Cassius, tears rolling down his face. "I'm not the person who you hurt anymore."

Hakon stepped forwards with some pills in his hand. "This is a blend to help your infection. King Myndill asked me to give them to you. He says he wants that fever gone as soon as possible."

He put them on the tray door and looked at Cassius expectantly. Cassius reluctantly took them, downing them with his glass of metallic water.

"Do you need any of your joints set before I leave?"

Cassius shook his head, surprised at the sudden change in attitude from Hakon. There were still tears in his eyes as he took back the tray.

"Make sure my water doesn't taste like piss tomorrow."

Cassius would never let Hakon off the hook at the end of the day.

That seemed to get under Hakon's skin. Cassius smiled as Hakon left without another word, the marks of his tears on the floor drying as he walked away.

— · —

Every alchemist had a maker. Now that Cassius thought about it, his life might not have been that different from Hakon's had he not been found by the right person.

Even if that part of his life was one hundred years ago, some institutions were immortal. Soup kitchens came to mind. Wherever people were, there was poverty. Where there was poverty, there was somewhere to feed the few impoverished lucky enough to make it in the door that day.

Times were different back then, weren't they? Though poverty always existed, the attitude changed over the years.

Back then, weren't they cruel? Cassius was just another orphan of the Tainted, after all. His family had all died by the time he was fifteen. Doomed to be nothing, Cassius hung in the soup kitchen as though it were a tavern. He was smart – if he volunteered to help with the cooking and cleaning and things nobody else wanted to do, they'd feed him first.

Nobody would hire an orphan of the Tainted with no skills. So, Cassius sought a way to have skills – the soup kitchen. If he could learn to cook, maybe he could find a home on a ship. He could be fed. He could do something. He might even *become* something.

That was until he met Janus. Janus came every day, without fail, to the soup kitchen. Cassius was long used to talking to the lonely souls that made up the soup kitchen's clientele, but Janus was different. Janus was as sharp as a razor. He had hopes and dreams. Janus gave Cassius energy in his quest to become *something*. Best of all, Janus didn't judge Cassius for being from a poor village. Things like that mattered back then, more than they did in the modern times.

One day, time seemed to freeze around them.

"You want to become something, don't you?"

Cassius had nodded frantically. Was it an offer of employment? Or was he about to be recruited into some underground organization?

"My dear, you have the makings of an alchemist."

The word sent fear down Cassius' spine at first. Alchemists weren't always good news. If this man was an alchemist, his very life could be in danger.

"You're brilliant. You've learned the streets as if you wrote the guidebook on survival out here. Yet I imagine you as someone who forges paths that lead to wonders beyond our imaginations, writing guidebook after guidebook. My boy, you could become more than something. You could become *great*."

Those were the words that sold Cassius on the deal. He'd do anything to become better than a something. The promise of a chance at greatness would've taken him anywhere.

Nothing would stop Cassius from becoming great. That youthful ambition never left him. It was ingrained into his very soul like the image of his family murdered by a wild Tainted.

Even in his worst days, it kept him going.

Now, Cassius began to wonder if it might have led him astray. If only Janus was still around to talk to. Maybe then, he'd know if he'd achieved that greatness.

*** 

Cassius' walls were crumbling more and more every day. Would he have embarked on this life if he knew that it would end with him strapped and tortured by the king of the creatures that had murdered his family?

Almost certainly.

Cassius wasn't dumb enough to believe that something that far ahead would've stopped him.

"You see, dear Cassius, I don't think those feet are doing you much good."

King Myndill was smiling wickedly at him. Cassius was strapped down to the table, per usual. The days of torture took all the health left in his body. Every morning, he was hardly able to move. The guards had needed to carry him to the torture room rather than having him walk. Maybe it was the mix of tonics and poisons that Myndill liked to feed him when he was misbehaving that was causing the fatigue. Regardless, Cassius was growing more and more concerned for the state of his body.

He could only hope that someone would rescue him from the pain before Myndill killed him.

"You experimented a lot on poor Hakon, right?" His tone was mocking as he circled Cassius, grinning. "Well, I've always wanted to do an experiment of my own. See, Cassius, I have quite an ability with the cold. I've always wondered what would happen if I used my magic to freeze the blood inside a person. What would happen to their cells? What type of pain would they experience?"

King Myndill got another one of his mock-caring faces on as he continued. "You see, I have quite a number of prisoners who come through here. You're different, of course. You're a toy of mine. I'll keep you until I get bored. Yet, because you're my toy, you make for the perfect test subject."

Myndill laid a hand on Cassius' strapped leg. "What do you say?"

Rage bubbled inside Cassius to cover the fear he was feeling. He knew better than Myndill did what that would do to him. Myndill must've known that too.

"Silent? That's new."

"You're mad. You're absolutely mad. I could lose my legs."

Myndill broke out laughing. "Good. Then you won't run."

Cassius growled, but it was quickly cut off as overwhelming pain filled his toes.

"We'll start small and move up."

The ice through his veins tore his flesh apart. His nerves snapped like thin threads as a million knives were being shoved through his skin, inside out.

He couldn't help it.

He screamed bloody murder.

"That much for just the beginning?"

Myndill clearly didn't understand that though his body could endure such things, Cassius was still human and had the limitations of a human body.

"Stop! Fucking stop!"

The pain as Myndill escalated, crawling up his foot, was so bad that he began to feel faint. He didn't want to give the bastard any pleasure from his fainting, but he wasn't sure he had much of a choice.

Stars began to form in his vision. How long would it last? It already felt like hours had passed, even if Cassius knew that to be impossible.

He didn't have much time to think as he let out another scream. The pain was moving up his leg. He could've sworn that his leg had torn open and was gushing blood. Nothing made sense anymore. He was slipping. His vision was darkening on the sides. Eventually, he felt that familiar pang of panicked dizziness before he slipped into unconsciousness.

*** 

Cassius awoke to the feeling of drowning. Something was over his face. He couldn't breathe.

Maybe the bastard had finally left him to die. It wasn't a thought that particularly bothered Cassius. Meeting his tragic end infuriated him, yes, but the idea of breaking under Myndill's grasp was more infuriating.

The cloth was yanked off of his face.

Myndill's black-edged eyes glared down at him.

"Hello there, sleeping beauty."

Cassius finally understood what was happening. It wasn't as though he'd never waterboarded anyone. He just didn't recognize the suffocating sensation until he was lifted out of that void.

"You're a monster! A fucking monster! I hate you. I hate your kind. You're all evil."

King Myndill's smile dropped as he looked at Cassius. "You have the audacity to call me a monster? *You*, of all people, Cassius?"

Cassius growled. "I didn't give in to Taint like you did."

A lupine growl escaped King Myndill's lips. His teeth were sharp, as were his horns. For a moment, Cassius could've sworn he saw the ghost of a wolf in Myndill, black ears, amber eyes, and tall form instead of that human that stood before him.

"And you think this world is fair, Cassius?" King Myndill snarled. "Do you think it's just that kind children like Hakon get outcasted for being so distraught and lost that they lose themselves to their emotions?"

Cassius narrowed his eyes and glared at King Myndill. "I care not what happens to orphan consumptives once they've served their purpose."

King Myndill backhanded Cassius. "And weren't you a poor orphan once too? Where is your empathy? By the Judge's name, you might've helped the world. Instead, you chose to torture *my* people. You chose to strap us down to tables, torture, and murder us. For what? Your own ambition?"

That flash of a wolf became clearer as Cassius watched Myndill hold back his own rage. "Do you think that would've brought you greatness?"

"Your kind are a blight on this world. *Your* kind murdered my family. Hakon was unwanted from the start. *I* had people who loved me. My research is more important than the lives of a few creatures too weak to hold up under pressure. I want to help heal people. Real people. Strong people. Not ones who'd easily give in to Taint. People like me who've had to endure and find a way in a world that didn't care. I want people to remember me."

Myndill released Cassius from his restraints for a moment, before his hands wrapped around his throat.

"Let me tell you something, Cassius."

His voice was a dangerous hiss.

"I was happy, once, too. I had people who loved me. But, you see, humans saw it fit to take that all away from me. I lived with my mother and father, my sisters, my brothers, and some others in a pack. I didn't always have this human form. I was once only a wolf, a fae creature, but still a wolf."

Cassius was struggling for air as Myndill was speaking. King Myndill was holding back to ensure that Cassius could still breathe, but squeezing the sides of his neck tight enough to leave bruises.

"I was their defender. We weren't wild wolves. One day, when I was away to look for one of my sisters who'd gone missing, humans came and murdered everyone. My sister's body was only the first I found. Every. Single. One. Murdered by humans.

"I felt so helpless. There was nothing I could do. The humans were long gone. Even then, murdering them would never bring my pack back. One day, I got the dream, and awoke in human form as a Tainted. I've kept both forms, though with years it gets harder to move between the two."

Myndill's hands squeezed tightly around Cassius' throat. "We never bothered humans. We never ate their livestock. So, why did they murder us?" Myndill squeezed a bit tighter. Cassius knew he couldn't last much longer. "I never held it against humankind the way you hold it against the Tainted."

Finally, Myndill let go. "This world isn't fair. There isn't divine justice. I only built this kingdom to repent for not being able to save them. People, *creatures* like you, are the ones that I need to defend my people from. I'm not the evil one. Like Hakon, I simply lost myself to my own soul's weakness. I'm happier here than I've ever been since losing my family. You will not ruin that because you naively believe in justice."

Myndill grabbed Cassius' arm and began to twist. The first snap was horrible and loud. Cassius screamed in pain, shouting, perhaps even begging, for King Myndill to stop.

"You will repent. You'll understand that it isn't strength that kept you from becoming Tainted. It was merely luck and privilege. I will break you. By the end of the week, you will be clay in my hands."

Myndill kept pulling on Cassius' arm. A second, then a third snap came as tears welled in Cassius' eyes.

"You will never be great. You'll always be a pathetic kid who never moved on."

The final snap of Cassius' shoulder breaking freed the tears in his eyes. For the first time in more years than he cared to count, Cassius cried true tears of agony.

"There will be many more tears for you, Cassius. I promise you that. You're going to regret the day that you decided to torture my people. You're going to regret every bad decision you've ever made. And you'll apologize. You'll apologize to Hakon personally and beg him for forgiveness."

Somehow, Cassius found a part of himself believing that he really would do all those things, no matter how much he resented the idea. No, Cassius couldn't even manage to smirk at the idea.

—·—

Cassius sneered when Elijah emerged from his room. "You look awful."

Elijah already knew it, but seeing the look of disgust on Cassius' face was still painful, even if he knew he should've been used to it. His eyes were sticky from his untreated allergies and his skin glittered from his consumptive night sweats. Some days, the weakness was worse than others. That day was one of the worst that Hakon could remember from his mortal life.

He dropped a knee to Cassius, bowing his head. He shook, though whether from the fatigue or the fear of him, Elijah didn't know.

"You may rise." Elijah could hear Cassius' smile in his voice.

Elijah immediately complied, keeping his gaze squarely on the ground and ensuring that he didn't look too large.

Cassius grabbed Elijah's chin and made him look up. "I like this version of you much better. So compliant. Quiet." Cassius tilted his head further up. Elijah didn't move except to allow Cassius to look at his neck. "You're losing a lot of weight."

The truth was that his weight loss wasn't entirely due to his consumption. Elijah seldom found the energy to eat. He'd resigned himself to dying, whether by his own hand, Cassius', or his disease's. There was no hope for him. Even if he somehow left, he would never have a life. He would never do anything. He was pathetic. He was weak. He allowed himself to be someone else's experimental toy. All the decisions he made were stupid. Yes, it would be better if he died.

"You probably don't have much longer."

Elijah's stomach sank. Even if he wished for death, it still scared him. He didn't want to die in that painful way that consumptives did.

Cassius put a hand to Elijah's forehead. "Bad fever. Yeah, kid, you don't have much longer."

The insouciant way that Cassius talked about his death scared him. *Maybe I can ask him to kill me. Maybe he would.*

"S-sir?"

"You may speak."

Cassius was annoyed. Elijah shrank, but not enough to make Cassius upset because he moved away from his touch.

"If – if you would be so kind, please kill me. I – you have to have the methods. I don't want to die of consumption."

Cassius seemed to seriously consider it for a moment. Elijah swallowed as Cassius moved his hand away from his forehead. He knew the slap was coming before it happened, but still cried after the sharp backhand.

"How *dare* you think of me as a murderer! I don't kill humans like that."

Elijah whimpered.

"Your use is coming to an end anyway."

Cassius threw him to the ground and kicked him hard in the side. "First you fail to fall to Taint, then you have the audacity to ask me to kill you. Since when have I cared about what you want?"

"Never, sir. I'm sorry, sir. Please. Please forgive me, sir. I can't go out there, sir."

Cassius glared down at him. "That's right. You won't survive out there. It *would* be like killing you to send you out there alone."

Elijah's whimpers turned into keening. He was fighting back tears.

"That's what you want, though, anyway."

Elijah froze. "Please, sir. Please, no, sir. I can't, sir."

"Silence!" Cassius shouted. He kicked Elijah even harder, throwing Elijah into a bloody, violent coughing fit.

"You asked for death. I'll fucking give it to you. On my terms."

\*\*\*

Cassius felt like he was going to die. Sure, he'd felt that yesterday when King Myndill had waterboarded, then choked him, but this, this was different.

Another wave of electricity crashed through his body. He let out a bloody scream.

Every muscle in his body ached. He wanted it all to stop.

Memories of that horrible day when lightning came from the sky at the will of that wretched Tainted came flooding back.

Suddenly, he found himself panicking.

He couldn't breathe.

He could smell the burning flesh.

Just as he continued to panic, a wave of electricity crashed through his body again. There were tears in his eyes as he heard the screams of his family. Suddenly, his screams seemed to be mixed with a phantasm of every scream they'd cried that day.

"This won't stop until you beg."

Myndill had paused with the shocks and instead gently wiped a tear from Cassius' eye.

"Come on. I know you can do it."

*No. No. He's going to –*

The next wave came with enough force to make his eyes roll to the back of his head. He thrashed in his restraints, bloody gashes cutting into his wrists and ankles. He was in so much pain. He couldn't take it anymore. He was going to die if he didn't do something. He couldn't even breathe.

A whip cracked down on him while the electricity raced through his body, leaving bloody, excruciating marks on his chest.

That was it.

It was all suddenly too much.

Cassius needed it to stop no matter what.

*Funny.*

*This is exactly how I broke Elijah.*

Just as Myndill threatened another wave worse than the last, Cassius finally gave up. Tears flowed freely from his eyes.

"Please, make it stop."

"I didn't hear that. What did you say?" Myndill touched the glowing orb he'd been using to generate the electricity.

Cassius knew exactly what he was looking for.

"Please, Liege, make it stop. I can't take it anymore. I'm too weak. Please, please, please, I'll do anything. Just make it stop. Just make it stop, please."

He was hysterical as Myndill threatened to electrocute him again.

"I can't take the screams. I can't take the memories. I need it all to stop."

A smile parted Myndill's lips. "You'll be obedient from now on?"

"Yes," Cassius replied with enthusiasm. "Yes. I'll be perfect and obedient, just please make it stop."

Myndill chuckled. "Well, then, I think we've made enough progress for today."

With relief beyond measure, Cassius watched Myndill release his restraints.

"Not so fast."

Cassius' heart sank as he sat up. Myndill grabbed his broken wrist with crushing force and pushed deep down on the broken bones, grinding them to a pulp and setting them further out of place. He'd managed to fix some of it with alchemy the previous night, but with each second that passed, Cassius doubted he'd be able to fix his wrist at all.

"I want you to remember this day. You're *mine*."

Myndill pushed him off the table using his broken arm, which made Cassius scream in pain.

"Guards! Get him back to his cell. Make sure Hakon gets him something to eat. He hasn't eaten in a day."

Cassius couldn't even be happy at the notion of food between his sobs.

***

Hakon didn't know what he would be greeted with when he heard that Cassius had finally broken. He thought back to when Cassius had broken him, what he had done. Hakon was sure he'd hidden in a closet and refused to eat for days.

Seeing Cassius hiding in the farthest corner of his cell, curled up in a ball with a clearly broken and disfigured arm hanging to the side and blood running down his wrists and ankles, was somehow not at all what he expected.

Something in him immediately was horrified.

*Why do I feel bad for him?*

The answer was easy – Hakon had morals. Cassius didn't. He was stronger than Cassius. He was *kinder* than Cassius.

Hakon pushed the tray of food through the door, but Cassius didn't respond. His head was turned to the side, his gaze not even looking at him for a second.

"Cassius?"

"Come to see me now that I'm broken?"

Hakon's heart fell when he heard the tears in Cassius' voice.

The truth was that Hakon had long forgiven the man. Sure, Cassius was a madman. Just another someone driven by something that Hakon would never understand. Nothing that had happened was Hakon's fault. Cassius singularly held that blame.

Hakon refused to hold on to the pain and allow Cassius to control his life. The only way that he knew to make that happen was to forgive what Cassius did, even if it was unforgivable, make peace with his own emotions, and move on.

Without resentment and an urge to take revenge, Hakon had been free to become Seer and make a life for himself. Did that mean that what Cassius did never bothered him? No. Did that mean that Hakon thought it was all justified? Definitely not. However, it meant freedom. A freedom he didn't have without it.

"Can someone get me bandages, cheap spirits, some leather, and some stiff wood?"

The guards quickly followed his orders. They brought what he had asked for with no question.

"Cassius, I'm going to take care of your wounds."

Cassius looked at Hakon with genuine shock in his eyes. Hakon knew that look well. Cassius had only expected cruelty, even from someone who'd never shown him any.

The look sent chills down his spine. He knew that he'd looked at everyone like that at the beginning. Seeing Cassius, the one who'd broken him, looking at him like that brought him no pleasure or joy. It simply made him ache. He'd have never wished that pain on anyone, even Cassius.

Hakon opened the cell door and entered quietly. He didn't really know where to start with tending to Cassius' wounds. He figured he'd start with his ankle gashes.

"I'm sorry for the pain, Cassius."

Cassius looked at him like he had no clue why Hakon was apologizing. Nonetheless, his hoarse whimpers started as Hakon gently poured alcohol onto the cuts and dabbed at them with gauze.

Once the dirt and old blood was cleared and he was sure the wound was disinfected, Hakon moved on to his bloodied and bruised wrists.

He lightly dabbed at the gash on his deformed wrist. The swelling caused the gash to open wider.

Gently, Hakon wrapped the wound in bandages.

"Will you be able to fix your shoulder and elbow with alchemy?"

To his absolute shock, Cassius shook his head. "The winds here are too hard to control. I can't do a good job."

Hakon just nodded in response. Quietly, despite the yelps and small screams from Cassius, he tied each joint straight with wood and leather. He gave small apologies the entire time he worked on Cassius.

Eventually, with tears in his eyes, Cassius looked at him. It took them a while to get through all the cuts that needed to be disinfected and covered. Then Hakon fed him carefully. He needed all the strength he could get. He had a difficult road of healing ahead of him.

Cassius didn't speak until Hakon was picking up the bloodied scrap bandages and the dirty dishes.

"Hey, Hakon?"

His voice was hoarse from the crying and screaming. Hakon found it deeply unsettling to hear the person who'd tortured him talk like that.

"Yeah?"

Cassius was silent for a really long time, before he finally got the courage to speak.

"I'm sorry for what I did to you."

Hakon didn't really know what to say. He didn't need Cassius' apology. He didn't even know if it was genuine or born out of self-pity. It was probably the latter, all things considered. Cassius never regretted anything. He only cared about himself. He probably thought that apologizing was better than saying "thank you" like a normal person.

"No apology will make up for what you did to me."

"I know."

Hakon left shortly after. He didn't know what to make of the conversation, so he didn't think about it. He needed to go complete his readings. He didn't have room in his mind to ponder *why* Cassius had apologized and what exactly King Myndill had done to break him so completely.

When he finally found himself ready to sit down to do his readings, he was simply too unsettled. Alfie brought him tea and the two of them talked about nothing.

For once, the smile came easily to Hakon's face as they talked about the snowfall that evening. Anything to get his mind off of what had happened with Cassius.

—·—

Sometimes, what Hakon saw in his readings was incomprehensible in the moment. Most of the time, Hakon found himself missing some important context that he didn't understand until he thought through similar jobs. Rarely, though, what he saw shook him so deeply that it took him time to be able to comprehend it.

It seemed that with Valentina, he was having more and more trouble comprehending her actions. He understood all the context. He'd kept surveillance on her for long enough to understand her modus operandi. However, the *why* of what she did was completely impossible to understand.

Dare he say that he might've found someone more heartless, more ruthless, than Cassius himself?

The image of having the woman invade his home and tear it all apart terrorized Hakon. He saw what she did to the areas she targeted. There was nothing left in her wake. She brutalized the dead bodies and hung heads from spears at the village gates.

Hakon would die. King Myndill would die. Alfie would die. Worst of all, he knew King Myndill to be too prideful to give up the fight now that he knew about it.

"Alfie?"

They came from the other room. "Hakon? What can I help you with?"

He put down the bones he was reading off of and pulled his blindfold off. "Can you get me some cloths and a glass of tea?"

Alfie raised an eyebrow. "Are you sure?"

Hakon nodded, looking at them with his sharp golden eyes.

They shrugged. They knew better than to question when the Seer wanted to stop with his readings.

They were quick to return with damp cloths. Hakon quietly wiped the ink off of his body, closing the link to the golden threads. It was something of a relief – sometimes, they were a rather overwhelming phenomenon. Too much information, too much going on to comprehend fully. It was perhaps best compared to trying to keep track of a thousand conversations – impossible, even for the sharpest minds.

Once Hakon was finished removing the ritual marks, Alfie put a hand on his shoulder.

"What's wrong?"

Hakon startled. "What do you mean?"

They looked at Hakon gently, kindly. "I can see on your face that something's wrong."

That much was true. To Alfie, Hakon was an open book. He just wasn't used to showing his emotions so obviously. Maybe his readings lowered his inhibitions. Or maybe it was just a comfort around them that he found so foreign he couldn't recognize that he was actually comfortable around someone.

"We can't fight Valentina," he blurted.

Alfie looked at him curiously. "What makes you say that?"

With a panicked edge to his voice, Hakon continued at their prompting. "She's awful. She kills everything in sight. Even if we beat her successfully, we'll lose too many people. His Majesty won't back down, though. I know he won't."

Alfie was quiet for a long time. "So, this alchemist is so powerful that we don't even really stand a chance?"

Hakon shook his head. "Our kingdom is too new. Our forces are not trained enough. Cohesive enough. Our territory is easy to defend, yes, but how many are we willing to lose over one prisoner?"

They watched him cautiously, motioning for him to continue.

"I think His Majesty would forgive me if I did what was best for his kingdom, even if it isn't the action he would take."

The images of bloodied battlefields flew through him. He couldn't allow the people he loved to be hurt in such a way. He'd have failed at his job as Seer – to make important decisions with knowledge of the past, present, and future, knowledge that only he had.

"I – " Hakon forced himself to take a deep breath and try to stay in the moment. "I hate what I have to do. I couldn't even describe what I saw to you. Just bodies covered in blood, decapitated, with limbs torn off."

"You know I'm always here by your side. My role is to support your decisions and to help you do what is right by this kingdom, not His Majesty. What is it that you want to do with your knowledge, Hakon?"

Alfie quietly pulled Hakon into a hug, just before grabbing one of their signature glasses of chamomile tea and handing it to him.

"I have to let Cassius go. I need him to go to the alchemists and tell them not to attack. They'll listen to him. I've seen how they respect him."

Alfie paused. "Are you sure?" Their voice was a whisper.

"Completely. I hate the idea too, but it's the only way to save this place. My home."

Alfie swallowed, then nodded. "I understand. Just let me know what I should do."

Hakon nodded, taking a deep sip of the tea. Tears were forming in his eyes as he looked down at it. "Why me?"

"Asking why is always futile in confronting helplessness. I don't like it either."

\*\*\*

Hakon quickly dismissed the guards from where Cassius was held. He needed total privacy for what he was about to do.

Cassius looked at him blankly when he arrived without food and made no comment. The absence of any of his snarky remarks unsettled Hakon beyond measure. Cassius' jaw hung open a little limply and he could see the remnants of tears on his face.

Suddenly, the idea that Cassius might not be able to run with him struck him. He was in horrible condition. *What am I getting myself into?*

"Cassius?"

"Yes?"

It was the most polite response he'd ever gotten from Cassius.

"I – we need to talk."

Cassius gave him a familiar, curious look. "About what?"

Hakon had a sad smile on his lips. "They're sending Valentina after you."

Hakon didn't know why he decided to be honest with Cassius. He had no reason to. All the cards were in his hand and to tell Cassius was to give him leverage in the negotiation. However, that human part of him that saw Cassius hurt wanted to speak to him as an equal about matters of life and death.

"She's going to rip this fucking place apart."

"I know. I saw it all." Hakon rubbed his hands together.

"What? You've come to ask me if I can call her off from here?"

"No." Hakon swallowed. "I have two choices right now: either have you work with His Majesty and arrange a counter defense against her, knowing that there's going to be a lot of casualties, or let you go and have you call off the offensive."

A small look of curiosity flashed across Cassius' face before it quickly disappeared under the immensity of his despair.

"Why should I help the Tainted creatures that tortured me?"

That was exactly the question that Hakon had anticipated and the one there was no easy answer for.

"I'll be honest. My reasons for releasing you are purely selfish. I want to preserve what's mine, not help you." Hakon took a deep breath. "However, I also know you want to make it out of here alive. So, we both win. You make the alchemists call off the offensive and take all of the blame. If you do that, I'll make sure you're left alone for the rest of your days."

Cassius seemed to seriously consider it. "Lie – King Myndill would let you do that?"

"He doesn't have to know, does he? Anyway, if you tell him, he'd never believe you over me."

Cassius nodded without argument. Again, Hakon was shocked.

"I don't want to owe Valentina anything." Cassius began to cough, but the bruising on his ribs was obvious. Hakon hoped that his broken ribs weren't too bad.

"Then be ready." Hakon swallowed. He didn't want to thank Cassius. Instead, he left quickly, calling the guards back and heading to speak to Alfie.

\*\*\*

Cassius couldn't believe that he was escaping. He wouldn't have to live through the torture soon. It seemed almost too good to be true. Nevertheless, if he knew one thing about Hakon, it was that Hakon wasn't a liar.

What a surprise it had been to see him here, healed and doing well for himself. The feeling it left Cassius with was almost indescribable. It was an odd mix between nostalgia, sadness, and victory. He'd succeeded. Seeing Hakon reminded him of a time when others didn't look down on him so much. However, his life had mostly stagnated, while Hakon's had exploded.

Cassius broke out in another coughing spell. Even if there were no clocks and no windows, he knew it was time for a meal soon.

Just as the thought crossed his mind, Hakon came down the stairs. *Hakon, right. Not Elijah.*

The two were becoming separate entities in his mind. Hakon was strong. Hakon might've been his equal in a different life. Elijah was pathetic. Elijah would always be inferior.

Hakon slid him his meal.

He picked at it a bit. There were questions on his mind that he couldn't leave the Tainted's kingdom without having an answer to, not after everything he'd been through with Hakon.

"Hakon, can I ask you something?"

For some reason, as he set his tray down, Cassius found himself somewhat afraid of the answers to what he was going to ask.

"Yes."

Hakon was curt.

"When I broke you, how was it?"

Hakon looked offended. Cassius hated the way he shrunk away from the angered face of the Tainted in front of him.

"Why the fuck do you want to know that?"

Cassius, with as genuine a voice as he could manage, answered simply. "For me, it happened within a moment. I just couldn't take it anymore. Suddenly, the price of holding on was too much. I had to give in."

Hakon, with thinly veiled hostility, was quiet for a long time. "It was the same for me. Suddenly, I couldn't resist *you* anymore. I couldn't stand up to *you*. Everything was too awful because of *you*."

The emphasis of his role in Hakon's torture wasn't lost on Cassius. "I'm sorry that my experiment failed."

"What? You're only sorry that your experiment failed? Not for the hell I went through?"

Cassius didn't doubt that answer for a moment. He went quiet while trying to think of a way to change the subject before he was forced to answer with something Hakon wouldn't like.

Hakon said, "We all fight at the beginning. We all want out. Eventually, we all realize it's never going to fucking happen. We realize that the pain is forever. We realize that we're going to die there, huh? You're lucky I've spared you. You're so lucky that I was kind to you. I have more strength than you ever will, Cassius. I have thousands of years ahead of me. You'll be a speck in my history, a bad one at that."

Cassius flinched a bit at the final bit of Hakon's rant. However, he didn't want to respond to that.

He stayed quiet as Hakon continued on his rant, allowing Hakon to dig into him for the first time. He did not have the mental strength to stop him. In some sick way, it made him feel better to know that Hakon was no saint. He was flawed, just like Cassius. His forgiveness was imperfect. He still harbored his anger and his flame.

*I always failed to extinguish it, huh?*

Yes, Cassius had failed in every way with Hakon.

Somehow, that comforted his broken soul. He'd been right in what he did, but at least when he failed, it wasn't the end for someone. At least Hakon had been able to make a life for himself.

— · —

Facing King Myndill the next day felt oddly final. Cassius imagined that it was more similar to being carried off to the gallows than the moment before freedom.

No, his mind would never be free. Never again. Not after knowing what he knew now about himself. Breaking for King Myndill, that first time where he begged King Myndill to stop, would haunt him forever. King Myndill would be there for what remained of his life – a phantasm of a time where he was, for a moment, breakable.

After all, he was only made of onyx. Hakon, well, he was made of diamond. Though difficult, one could shatter onyx. Diamond, on the other hand, was unbreakable.

Hakon had never truly broken, Cassius suspected. He'd failed from the outset. Nothing would break Hakon if he couldn't break him. Cassius was strong, but Hakon was stronger. Accepting the fact that he had been bested by someone he'd looked down on for so long was difficult.

Being strapped to the same board every day made the torture feel routine, even if it carried that finality of being bested.

"You're awfully tame today, Cassius."

King Myndill wore a wicked smile that made Cassius' stomach knot. How was he to respond to such a question? King Myndill had left him alone for a few days. It seemed like mercy back then, but Cassius was left to wonder if he'd been devising some sort of horrible plan for his next tortures.

He had so many things he wanted to say. *You broke me, remember? That's what happens after weeks of torture. What did you expect?*

However, he knew that saying something like that would only earn him more pain. He wasn't stupid. He wouldn't put himself in danger for an insult, not anymore.

"Quiet. I think I like that." King Myndill hung over him, his black-edged eyes burning into him. "In fact, I've had something of a headache today. I think I need you to *stay* quiet."

King Myndill went over to one of his drawers and pulled out a thick cloth and muzzle.

"I've always had a hatred for these things." King Myndill walked over with the muzzle and thick cloth. "Humans used them against my kind for so long that when I see one, I'm filled with anger."

King Myndill grabbed Cassius' jaw and pushed until Cassius was tearing up with pain. The force slacked his jaw and King Myndill stuffed the cloth in his mouth.

"However." King Myndill began to tie the muzzle on Cassius' face, locking his jaw around the cloth. "Seeing it on a human? That makes me happy. Especially one as despicable as you."

Cassius felt himself folding inside as the muzzle's last strap was secured and King Myndill stepped back to admire his work. He hated the proud way that King Myndill gazed upon him, like a project that had finally gone right.

*I must've looked at Hakon like that. I wonder if he hated it so much.*

*He probably did.*

*Good.*

After all, it was the natural order of the world. He was strong, stronger than King Myndill, so he would escape after being the toy of the weaker creature. However, Hakon was stronger and thereby the one to rescue him. To be so powerful, he needed the pressure that Cassius had put him under – back when he was weak.

There was always a fire going in the room. However, today, there were hot rods in the fire. King Myndill, without being burned by them, picked one up from the fire and moved over to Cassius.

"I think we'll use these today. It's been a while since I branded you." He ran a gentle, caressing hand over Cassius' brand.

Of course, Cassius couldn't say a thing in response. He could only accept the pain. That had been the plan, anyway, but somehow, when the poker hit the soles of his feet, the pain of forced silence amplified the pain of flesh blistering.

*** 

"Dammit!"

Hakon wanted to scream when he saw the burn marks on the soles of Cassius' feet. He'd lined everything up for the escape to happen once King Myndill was satisfied with his toy for the day. He hadn't anticipated that King Myndill might burn Cassius' feet as part of his fun.

Cassius had flinched back when Hakon had shouted. That was definitely new.

"Fucking hell ... "

There was a slight tremor in Cassius' hands. "I-I'm sorry. I should've tried to stop him."

"No, you shouldn't have." Hakon shook his head. "I just didn't expect him to do this so early on ... without provocation."

Hakon remembered how he was around yelling in the beginning. He realized that he should definitely calm down to avoid scaring Cassius and making the whole situation harder on him.

*Scaring Cassius.* Hakon would have chuckled at the thought had the situation not been so dire.

"Could he have known?"

Hakon shook his head. The genuine, unadulterated fear in Cassius' voice scared him. "There's no way."

Hakon needed to be the confident one for this all to work.

"Did His Majesty use his magic on you at all, Cassius?"

Cassius seemed to go distant for a moment before he answered with a simple nod. That sparked some hope in Hakon. Maybe, just maybe, if the wounds had been made worse by manipulation magic, he could revert Cassius' skin back to its original state.

"You – you're Western-bound, right? You should be able to use restoration magic, right?"

Cassius was desperate. That much was obvious.

"I am, but I have no skill outside eclairer. Let me try something."

Hakon approached Cassius quietly and closed his eyes. He always had a connection to those threads, but they were hazier when he wasn't connected through ritual.

Those shadows of golden threads were tangled around Cassius' feet. Hakon knew immediately what to do.

As he began to manipulate the threads and straighten them out, Cassius began to scream and cry in pain. It was almost like Hakon was giving Cassius stitches without any pain medicine.

"Hold on, Cassius. I need you to stay conscious." Hakon offered Cassius his hand. "Hold on to me. It's okay."

Cassius immediately took hold of Hakon's hand. He gripped until Hakon thought that blood flow was cut off to his hand.

However, the healing was done quickly. The relief of the end was tangible for them both.

***

Nothing stopped Cassius. Elijah had learned that the hard way early on, but after a few years with the man, it was a lesson easily forgotten. After all, the suffering he thought was abhorrent in the beginning had become somewhat mundane. Of course Cassius would torture him. It was what Cassius did.

However, after realizing that, though Cassius was intent on not murdering him, he still wanted to be the cause of Elijah's death.

Walking out that day, in the cheapest clothes that Cassius had bought him, was like walking to the gallows.

He would never return to the lab. Somehow, it brought him no relief. See, Elijah had come to understand one simple truth: there was no life for him outside the lab. He would simply be left to die.

"Please, Cassius! I don't want to die."

Elijah had been hysterical when he saw the village that Cassius was going to be dropping him off at.

"Do you think I care?" Cassius towered over Elijah, making Elijah shrink in his skin. "Do you really think that after you ruined my experiment and attempted to end your own life, that

I can really believe that you *don't* want to die? That I should care about what you want?"

Elijah looked up at him in horror. "Please."

Cassius threw Elijah to the ground and hooked a sharp punch across his jaw. "Silence. You'll need to walk the rest of the way there yourself."

Elijah looked at Cassius with horrible fear in his eyes. "Please. Please! No."

Another hard punch in the same spot. There were tears in Elijah's eyes.

"Start walking. Don't you dare follow me back," Cassius growled.

Then, just as quickly as he'd come into Elijah's life, Cassius walked away for the last time. Elijah had laid there, alone, on the ground for a while before he finally decided to get up. He only had one option that day – forwards. He either died there or tried to create a life for himself now that he was no longer Cassius' captive.

Though nobody stood by his side, Elijah still had himself. Despite everything, that day, he'd decided to move forwards and see what his life would bring him, even if that was just more misery.

***

The border villages were never rich. As such, they were always riddled with crime and fear the moment a Tainted stepped foot into them. It was the perfect place to drop Cassius off. Everyone would turn a blind eye to his presence. He could recover some strength before he contacted the alchemists again, now that he was out of the Tainted's territory.

Being together with Cassius, staring down the village in the distance, was perhaps an all-too-familiar scene.

Cassius was struggling to stay on his feet, but he was holding together well enough.

"Hakon?"

Hakon looked at Cassius curiously. "Yes?"

Cassius began to cough. Hakon thought he might be choking until he put his head in his sleeve. The fit lasted a rather long time – long enough for Hakon to worry.

"Do you remember, a few days before I abandoned you, that you attempted to take your life? You said that you didn't want to die by my hands?"

Hakon froze a little. "How could I forget?"

Cassius swallowed, his chest uncomfortable. "I told you that day that it would be on my terms that you would die or not at all."

Hakon nodded solemnly. "Then I didn't end up dying at all. I became Tainted. I'm practically immortal now."

"Well, I'm not." Cassius swallowed again. He was sweating a bit. "Life has a bitter sort of irony, Hakon. I genuinely believed back then that you couldn't give me your consumption, that I was immune."

Cassius broke out in another coughing fit. "You'll end up killing me by circumstance, not the other way around." Blood tinged his sleeve.

"What do you mean?" There was a nervous edge to Hakon's voice. *Did he catch it?*

"You gave me your consumption." Cassius looked at him with the most gentle look he'd ever seen from the man. "I don't know how many years I have left. The doctor told me maybe five if I'm lucky."

Hakon had no idea what to say. He simply froze as Cassius took those few steps towards the village ahead of them.

"What I wanted to say to you, Hakon, is have a good life. Don't worry too much about me." Cassius smiled back at him, now a few paces ahead on the path to the village. "I know you will. I don't deserve your worry. I don't need it, either."

Hakon stood there, stunned, watching Cassius walk away into the sunset, towards the village he'd get to call home until the alchemists came for him.

When he got back, King Myndill had already found out. Once Hakon's reasoning came out with Alfie's help, King Myndill was quick to forgive him.

That didn't stop Hakon, over the next few days, from feeling empty, like a failure somehow. He'd let Cassius have the last word, again. He'd let Cassius walk away, again. Still, after all those years, Cassius could make him go silent.

Cassius held to his word. The alchemists never attacked. The threads gave no indication of any such thing.

Still, even weeks after King Myndill had found his next toy, Hakon was left to wonder whether having that last word would've changed the hollowness of knowing how weak that man from his past really was.

Probably not, Hakon concluded.

But it would've felt good.

# ABOUT THE AUTHOR

Harper is a long-time writer turned whump enthusiast. She enjoys a variety of different types of whump and likes to not leave any genre unturned. She has a love for fantasy and combines intricate soft worldbuilding with hurt to create stories that explore the human and nonhuman condition. She also has a love for surrealism. Though a private person, Harper incorporates parts of her life in her stories to create pieces that she hopes are both comforting and difficult to read at times.

## BEFORE YOU GO

This is the twelfth and final book in 12 Months of Whump, a
series of whumpy novellas published by WPP throughout 2025.
Each novella can be read as a standalone.
To stay up to date with other whumperfly-inducing projects,
visit us at
https://thewhumpyprintingpress.tumblr.com/